Twenty-Ninth Annual Report of the Resident Physician of the Belfast District Hospital for the Insane Poor

Anatiposi

Anonymous

Twenty-Ninth Annual Report of the Resident Physician of the Belfast District Hospital for the Insane Poor

Reprint of the original.

1st Edition 2023 | ISBN: 978-3-38230-484-3

Anatiposi Verlag is an imprint of Outlook Verlagsgesellschaft mbH.

Verlag (Publisher): Outlook Verlag GmbH, Zeilweg 44, 60439 Frankfurt, Deutschland
Vertretungsberechtigt (Authorized to represent): E. Roepke, Zeilweg 44, 60439 Frankfurt, Deutschland
Druck (Print): Books on Demand GmbH, In de Tarpen 42, 22848 Norderstedt, Deutschland

TWENTY-NINTH ANNUAL REPORT

OF

THE RESIDENT PHYSICIAN

OF THE

BELFAST DISTRICT

Hospital for the Insane Poor

OF THE

COUNTIES OF ANTRIM AND DOWN, AND THE COUNTY OF THE TOWN OF CARRICKFERGUS,

From 1st April, 1858, to the 31st March, 1859.

ESTABLISHED 1829.

BELFAST:
PRINTED AT THE "NORTHERN WHIG" OFFICE,
CALENDER STREET.

1859.

CONTENTS OF REPORT.

CONTENTS OF APPENDIX (No. 1.)

CONTENTS OF APPENDIX (No. 2.)

GOVERNORS

OF

The Belfast District Hospital for the Insane,

APPOINTED BY

THE LORD LIEUTENANT AND PRIVY COUNCIL OF IRELAND,

Under the Provisions of 1 and 2 George IV. Cap. 33.

No.	NAME.	RESIDENCE.	DATE OF APPOINTMENT.
1	Marquis of Donegall,	London,	March, 1829.
2	Mayor of Belfast for the time being		March, 1829.
3	Rev. Thomas Hincks, A.M.,	Derrykeighan Rectory, Dervock,	March, 1829.
4	Sir Robert Bateson, Bart., D.L.,	Belvoir Park, Belfast,	June 28, 1829.
5	William M'Cance, Esq., J.P.,	Belfast,	Jan. 4, 1836.
6	Robt. J. Tennent, Esq., J.P., D.L.,	Belfast,	Jan. 4, 1836.
7	Edward Bruce, Esq., J.P.,		Oct. 28, 1836.
8	Right Rev. C. Denvir, D.D.,	Belfast,	Oct. 28, 1836.
9	Rev. John Edgar, D.D.,	Belfast,	Oct. 28, 1836.
10	Rev. H. Montgomery, LL.D.,	Dunmurry,	Oct. 28, 1836.
11	Very Rev. Dean Stannus,	Lisburn,	April 4, 1842.
12	Rev. H. Cooke, D.D., LL.D.,	Belfast,	April 4, 1842.
13	Rev. J. S. B. Monsell, A.M.,		July 13, 1842.
14	Conway B. Grimshaw, Esq.,	Belfast,	Oct. 8, 1846.
15	John Clarke, Esq., J.P.,	Belfast,	Sept. 13, 1847.
16	Marquis of Downshire,	Castle, Hillsborough,	Nov. 16, 1847.
17	Robt. Gordon, Esq., J.P., D.L.,	Florida Manor, Killinchy,	Nov. 16, 1847.
18	Robert Batt, Esq., J.P., D.L.,	Purdysburn, Belfast,	Nov. 16, 1847.
19	Major John S. Crawford, J.P.,	Crawfordsburn, Holywood,	Nov. 16, 1847.
20	Lord Bishop of Down & Connor & Dromore, for the time being	The Palace, Holywood,	April 9, 1850.
21	William Dunville, Esq., J.P.,	Richmond Lodge,	May 22, 1851.
22	Rev. T. F. Miller, A.M.,	Vicarage, Belfast,	Dec. 8, 1851.
23	Adam J. Macrory, Esq,	Duncairn, Belfast,	June 15, 1852.
24	Lord Dufferin,	Clandeboye, Holywood,	Dec. 10, 1855.
25	Thomas M'Clure, Esq., J.P.,	Belmont,	Jan. 29, 1856.

*** The two Government Inspectors, Drs. Nugent and Hatchell, are *ex-officio* members of the Board.

Resident Physician,		ROBERT STEWART, M.D.
Visiting Physician,		HENRY M'CORMAC, M.D.
Visiting Surgeon, &c.,		JAMES MOORE, M.D.

STATED MEETINGS OF GOVERNORS ARE HELD IN THE BOARD-ROOM ON THE FIRST MONDAY OF EACH MONTH AT ONE O'CLOCK, P.M.

The Belfast District Hospital for the Insane,

FOR THE YEAR ENDED 31st MARCH, 1859.

Table I.—General Statements of the year's admissions, &c.

	Males.	Females.	Total.	Males.	Females.	Total.
In House, on 1st April, 1858,		...	...	193	151	344
Admitted since, New Cases,	56	52	108			
Relapses,	1	5	6			
	—	—	—	57	57	114
Total under Treatment during the year,			...	250	208	458
Discharged, Recovered, ...	33	32	65			
Do., Relieved, ...	7	11	18			
Died, ...	12	6	18			
	—	—	—	52	49	101
Leaving in the House, 31st March, 1859,			...	198	159	357
The total Admissions during the year, were			...	57	57	114
Do. for the preceeding year,		...	...	71	76	147
Daily Average Number of Patients during the year, ...				...	...	347.21
Do. for the preceding year,		...	...	...	...	342.59
Average Annual Expense of each Patient for the past year, including every charge, ...					£19 8	2
Do. for the year ending 31st March, 1858, ...				...	17 3	10
Being an increase of each Patient this year of				...	2 4	4
Total Expenditure for the year ending 31st March, 1859,					6,738 18	2
Do. for the year ending 31st March, 1858,					5,889 16	7

"Dangerous Lunatics" admitted during the year, viz. :—

	Males.	Females.	Total.	Males.	Females.	Total.
From Antrim Gaol, ...	7	4	11			
From Down Gaol, ...	10	6	16			
	—	—	—	17	10	27

Produce of Farm and Garden, ...	...	...	...	£359 18	4
Deduct Farm and Garden Expenses, ...	...	...		55 8	7
Nett Profit,	...	...	...	£304 9	9

Table II.—Ages of the 114 Patients admitted during the year ended 31st March, 1859.

	Males	Females.	Total.
Under 20 years, ...	4	3	7
" 20 to 30 years, ...	13	19	32
" 30 to 40 "	14	14	28
" 40 to 50 "	13	14	27
" 50 to 60 "	9	5	14
" 60 to 70 "	3	2	5
" 70 to 80 "	1	0	1
TOTALS, ...	57	57	114

Table III.—Alleged Causes of Insanity in the 114 cases admitted during the year ended 31st March, 1859,

	Males.	Females.	Total.
Abuse of Medicine, ...	1	0	1
Apoplexy, ...	0	1	1
Bodily Ailments, ...	4	3	7
Disappointed Love,...	0	2	2
Epilepsy, ...	1	0	1
Excessive Study, ...	1	0	1
Fear of Want, ...	0	0	0
Fright, ...	3	2	5
Grief, Disappointment, and Anxiety, ...	4	7	11
Intemperance, ...	8	3	11
Puerperal Condition, ...	0	1	1
Paralysis, ...	1	0	1
Religious Excitement, ...	2	1	3
Unknown or Hereditary, ...	7	5	12
Totally Unknown, ...	25	32	57
TOTALS, ...	57	57	114

Table IV.—Forms of Insanity in the 114 cases admitted during the year ended 31st March, 1859.

	Males.	Females.	Total.
Dementia, ...	1	1	2
Mania, ...	44	34	78
Melancholia, ...	7	14	21
Monomania,...	5	8	13
TOTALS, ...	57	57	114

Table V.—Religion of the 114 cases admitted during the year ended 31st March, 1859.

	Males.	Females.	Total.
United Church of England and Ireland, ...	14	22	36
Presbyterians and Protestant Dissenters,...	26	21	47
Roman Catholics, ...	17	14	31
TOTALS, ...	57	57	114

Table VI.—Social Condition of the 114 cases admitted during the year ended 31st March, 1859.

	Males.	Famales.	Total.
Married, ...	20	16	36
Single, ...	36	37	73
Widowers and Widows, ...	1	4	5
TOTALS, ...	57	57	114

Table VII.—Occupation of the 114 cases admitted during the year ended 31st March, 1859.

	Males.	Females.	Total.
Barber,	1	0	1
Bleacher,	1	1	2
Carpenter,	1	0	1
Clerk,	1	0	1
Cardriver,	2	0	2
Cook,	0	1	1
Dealer,	1	0	1
Engineer,	1	0	1
Farmers, and Wives and Daughters of do.,	7	2	9
Flowerers and Sewers,	0	10	10
Gilder,	1	0	1
Gardener,	1	0	1
Housekeeper,	0	8	8
House Servants,	0	11	11
Labourers and Labourers Wives,	13	2	15
Mill Workers,	2	3	5
Paupers,	0	3	3
Sailors,	3	0	3
Schoolmaster and School Mistresses,	1	2	3
Saddlers,	2	0	2
Shoemaker,	2	0	2
Shopman,	2	0	2
Sawyer,	1	0	1
Spinner,	0	1	1
Tidewaiter,	1	0	1
Washerwoman,	0	1	1
Weavers,	11	3	14
Without any Occupation,	2	9	11
Totals,	57	57	114

Table VIII.—Degree of Education in the 114 cases admitted during the year ended 31st March, 1859.

	Males.	Females.	Total.
Well Educated,	3	2	5
Can Read and Write,	39	25	64
Can Read only,	8	19	27
Totally Uneducated,	7	11	18
Totals,	57	57	114

Table IX.—Ages of the 65 Patients discharged Recovered during the year
ended 31st March, 1859.

					Males.	Females.	Total.
Under 20 Years,	...	...	...	...	5	3	8
From 20 to 30 Years,	...	...	...	...	6	9	15
" 30 to 40 "	...	...	...	...	10	9	19
" 40 to 50 "	...	...	...	..	8	6	14
" 50 to 60 "	...	...	...	...	3	4	7
" 60 to 70 "	...	...	...	...	0	1	1
" 70 to 80 "	...	...	...	...	1	0	1
TOTALS,	...	...	...	...	33	32	65

Table X.—Shewing the period of time the 65 Patients discharged Recovered
were under treatment during the year ended 31st March, 1859.

					Males.	Females.	Total.
Under 3 Months,	..	...	...	...	11	9	20
From 3 to 6 Months,	...	...	...	...	8	10	18
" 6 to 12 "	...	...	...	...	6	8	14
" 1 to 2 Years,	...	...	...	...	5	3	8
" 2 to 5 " ...	...	...	...	...	2	2	4
" 5 to 10 " ...	...	...	...	...	1	0	1
TOTALS,	...	...	...	...	33	32	65

Table XI.—Shewing the Duration of Insanity in the 101 Patients discharged,
Recovered, and Relieved, and who Died during the year ended March 31, 1859.

DURATION OF INSANITY.	RECOVERED AND RELIEVED.			DIED.		
	Males.	Females	Total.	Males.	Females	Total.
Under 3 Months, ...	8	3	11	1	1	2
From 3 to 6 Months,	9	10	19	0	2	2
" 6 to 12 "	6	11	17	2	2	4
" 1 to 2 Years,...	10	7	17	2	0	2
" 2 to 5 "	5	6	11	2	1	3
" 5 to 10 "	2	5	7	1	0	1
" 10 to 20 "	0	0	0	2	0	2
" 20 to 28 "	0	1	1	2	0	2
TOTALS, ...	40	43	83	12	6	18

Table XII.—Ages of the 18 Patients who Died during the year ended 31st
March, 1859.

					Males.	Females.	Total.
Under 20 Years,	...	...	...	...	0	0	0
From 20 to 30 Years,	...	...	...	...	3	3	6
" 30 to 40 "	...	...	...	...	2	2	4
" 40 to 50 "	...	...	...	...	0	1	1
" 50 to 60 "	...	...	...	...	3	0	3
" 60 to 70 "	...	...	...	...	2	0	2
" 70 to 80 "	...	...	...	...	2	0	2
TOTALS,	...	...	...	...	12	6	18

Table XIII.—Employment during the year ended 31st March, 1859.

	Males.	Females.	Total.
Assisting Servants, ...	12	13	25
Basket-making,	2	0	2
Breaking Freestone,	6	0	6
Cultivating the Farm,	80	0	80
Embroidering,	0	8	8
Gardening Labour, ...	6	0	6
Knitting,	4	16	20
Making and Repairing Clothing, Bedding, &c., ...	4	14	18
Making and Repairing Shoes,	1	0	1
Painting,	1	0	1
Pumping Water,	30	0	30
Quilting,	0	4	4
Smith Work,...	2	0	2
Spinning,	0	20	20
Sweeping Yards, Carrying Coals, &c.,	20	0	20
Tailoring,	3	0	3
Washing in Laundry,	0	20	20
Weaving, Winding, and Warping, ...	8	0	8
TOTALS,	179	95	274

Table XIV.—Forms of Insanity of the Total Number of Patients remaining in the Hospital on 31st March, 1859.

	Males.	Females.	Total.
Dementia,	13	16	29
Mania,	123	78	201
Do., complicated with Epilepsy,	14	6	20
Monomania,...	17	25	42
Melancholia,	31	34	65
TOTALS,	198	159	357

Table XV.—Shewing the State of the Cases remaining in the Hospital on 31st March, 1859.

	Males.	Females.	Total.
Considered Chronic or Incurable Cases, ...	146	84	230
Probably Curable, ...	52	75	127
TOTALS,	198	159	357

Table XVI.—Shewing the Religious Persuasions of the 357 Patients Remaining in the Hospital on 31st March, 1859.

	Males.	Females.	Total.
United Church of England and Ireland, ...	60	53	113
Presbyterians,	73	50	123
Roman Catholics, ...	57	52	109
Unitarians, ...	4	1	5
Covenanters,...	3	0	3
Methodists, ...	0	3	3
Quaker,	1	0	1
TOTALS,	198	159	357

Table XVII.—Obituary for the year ended 31st March, 1859.

No.	Sex.	Age.	Form of Insanity and supposed Exciting Cause.	Social State.	Occupation.	Period an Inmate.	Cause of Death.
1	M.	26	Dementia—Unknown.	Single.	Pauper.	19½ months.	Phthisis.
2	F.	28	Mania—Unknown.	Single.	Flowerer.	11 days.	Exhaustion from Acute Mania.
3	F.	28	Mania—Religious Excitement.	Not known.	Servant.	6 months.	Maniacal Exhaustion.
4	F.	44	Mania—Natural Excitability.	Single.	Flowerer.	7 weeks.	Do.
5	F.	31	Mania—Suddenly frightened.	Married.	Flowerer.	13 months.	Do.
6	F.	35	Mono-Mania, Hereditary tendency.	Married.	Housewife.	7 days.	Suicide.
7	M.	79	Mania—Poverty.	Married.	Labourer.	9¼ years.	Apoplexy.
8	M.	26	Mania—Unknown.	Single.	Labourer.	2¾ years.	Epilepsy.
9	M.	54	Dementia—Pecuniary Losses.	Single.	Constabulary Pensioner.	20 months.	Paralysis.
10	M.	29	Mania—Loss of Land.	Single.	Labourer.	26 days.	Dysentery.
11	M.	50	Mania—Unknown.	Married.	Labourer.	21 days.	General Debility.
12	M.	50	Mania—Intemperance.	Married.	Saddler.	5½ months.	Paralysis.
13	M.	35	Mania—Hereditary Tendency.	Single.	Labourer.	11¼ years.	Phthisis.
14	M.	73	Mania—Unknown.	Married.	Labourer.	28 years.	Dropsy.
15	M.	66	Mania—Intemperance.	Single.	Tobacco Spinner.	20¼ years.	Dropsy.
16	M.	38	Mania—Unknown.	Single.	Labourer.	14 years & 10 months.	Epilepsy.
17	M.	66	Mania—Intemperance.	Married.	Farmer.	3½ months.	Paralysis.
18	M.	28	Mania—Hereditary Tendency.	Single.	Sailor.	2¾ years.	Scrofula.

GENERAL HEALTH.

The general state of health which prevailed amongst the inmates during the past year was of an unusually high standard, no serious illness of any kind having occurred, and those cases which required medical or surgical treatment being of the most ordinary and comparatively trifling nature; a condition of things, it is needless to say, of incalculable moment in such an institution, and calling for the expression of much thankfulness.

MORTALITY.

During the year, with an average daily number of patients of 347.21, the entire mortality was only eighteen, twelve males and six females, being under six per cent., whereas anything below 11 or 12 per cent. is considered a low average. The deaths for the preceding year (very few also), were twenty-five, with an average daily number of 342, so that in every point of view this year's mortality was exceedingly small indeed. The causes of death were—viz., maniacal exhaustion, four (females); paralysis, three (females) ; epilepsy, two (males) ; dropsy, two (males) ; general debility, two (males); pulmonary consumption, two (a male and female) ; apoplexy, one (male) ; dysentery, one (male).

One case of suicide occurred during the year, that of a female, aged 38, an inmate a week only, and who thus terminated her existence, after retiring to rest, between night and morning, by suspending herself, by means of the sheet of her bed, from the ventilator of her room. Before her admission she attempted self-destruction by cutting her throat. An inquest was held on the body, by J. K. Jackson, Esq., the District Coroner, and a verdict returned according to the above facts, no blame being attributed by the jury to any party, the unhappy event being just one of those cases which no ordinary human foresight could have prevented. The oldest of the death cases (a male), had reached the advanced age of 79, and had been an inmate nine and a quarter years. Another, aged 73, a male also, had been twenty-eight years and upwards in the house. A third male, aged 66, completed a residence of twenty-nine years. A fourth male, nearly 15 years. The average age of the males was 49, the oldest being, as above stated, 79, and the youngest 26. The average age of the females 32, the oldest being 44, and the youngest 26. The longest inmateship of any of the latter did not exceed 18 months, and the others were under treatment for periods varying from one year to one week.

SUICIDAL AND HOMICIDAL CASES.

Of the above classes who became inmates during the year now terminated, twenty-five (eight males and seventeen females), were suicidally disposed; and fifteen (nine males and six females), had a homicidal tendency. Of the suicidals, four (one male and three females), made actual attempts at self-destruction before their admission by strangulation; three (females), by submersion; three (females), by cutting the throat, precipitation from a window, and poison respectively.

ACCOMMODATION DURING THE YEAR.

The same report has to be made on this head as last year—namely, that throughout the entire year every available space was fully occupied—even beds were put into the attendants' rooms, that could accommodate them, in order to admit the press of cases, with the least possible delay, which were passed by the Board, and still it was impossible to receive all the applicants. At the present time the house is filled to the utmost—considerably overcrowded in fact, and five cases in ordinary are on the books for admission, as vacancies may arise, independently of several committed to the gaols of the district as "Dangerous Lunatics," under warrant of the Lord Lieutenant, there to be detained until they can be transmitted here.

FIRE IN THE LAUNDRY.

In the month of August last, a serious fire occurred in the drying closet attached to the Laundry, and before it could be extinguished much damage resulted, the flames having rapidly increased to a most alarming extent. The closet, which was heated by hot air pipes, was full of dried clothes at the time, and some portions of them having come in contact with the stove which had gotten overheated, the entire contents of the closet were immediately in flames. The damage sustained was under £300, and was fully covered by insurance. This very important department of the Institution, as erected by the authority

of the Board of Public Works, was never sufficiently adequate
to meet the wants of so large an establishment, and, accordingly,
the Governors, after much consideration, resolved not to restore
it as originally planned, but to supplement the proceeds arising
from insurance, by erecting Laundry buildings sufficiently
spacious, with a better, more economical, and a safer
system of drying through the means of steam. This
new department is only just now come into operation, and
from the trial made of it, every satisfaction has been given,
and, no doubt, will continue to be afforded, especially as regards the facility of drying, which has been greatly improved
and simplified, with a considerably increased space for that
purpose, thus adding to the domestic comfort and convenience
of the House to an incalculable extent.

SUPPLY OF WATER.

To the present time, the water required for the purposes of
the establishment has been raised by a force pump by the
labour of the patients. During the year now ended, the subject
of erecting a steam-engine for pumping was again under special
consideration, and, in fact, is still prominently before the Board.
It is considered that this description of work is more or less
objectionable for patients—not so much, however, from its
fatiguing as its monotonous nature. But on this head, it may
be observed, that several of the inmates are so accustomed to
this species of employment—one which is more in appearance
than in reality of a questionable character—that they would
do nothing else, and, consequently, would so far suffer from
the disuse of pumping. Still, as the consumption of water
is very large, a steam-engine would be of importance, in the
event of water from the town not being obtainable on
advantageous terms, but which, it is to be hoped, it may, as
under all the circumstances of the case, and taking into account
the local difficulties and inconveniences in the way of erecting a
steam-engine, would, unquestionably, be the more desirable
and certain mode of having this essential element always and
liberally at command.

REPORT OF THE COMMISSIONERS APPOINTED TO INQUIRE INTO THE
STATE OF THE LUNATIC ASYLUMS IN IRELAND.

In November last a copy of this report was laid before the
Board of Governors, together with a copy of Dr. Nugent's
observations thereon, as published in a letter addressed to Lord
Naas, the Chief Secretary to the Lord Lieutenant. Recently,
the Board having discovered that some mistakes of a very serious
nature against the administration of this Institution were contained in the Commissioners' Report, in respect of the consumption of certain articles of food, the subject was brought
under the special notice of the Lord Lieutenant, and subsequently
before the House of Commons. The correspondence and proceedings on that head will be found embodied in the appendix
to this report.

"LUNATIC POOR (IRELAND) BILL."

In February last a copy of this Bill, as introduced into the
House of Commons by Lord Naas and the Attorney-General for
Ireland, was laid before the Board, the same having been drawn
up in a great measure, according to the recommendations contained in the Report of the Commissioners of Inquiry, as above
referred to. The proceedings of the Board in connexion with
it are also herewith annexed.

The Bill in question is exceedingly novel and obnoxious
in many of its provisions, and proposes changes in the existing
well-understood system of government of the Irish District
Hospitals for the Insane, which are of an exceedingly
problematical nature, but into which this would not be the
place to enter. It may be observed, however, that so far as
regards the duties and position of the Chief Officer of those
establishments—the Physician-Superintendent—the provisions
of the Bill are most coercive, and to a large degree
derogatory. There are no fewer than seven penal clauses in
it directly affecting the Superintendent, the penalties varying
from two pounds to twenty pounds, and independently of these
special penal clauses in the Bill itself, power is given to the
Lord Lieutenant " to annex such penalties as he may think fit."
Besides those harsh and humiliating provisions, authority is
given to any single "visiter" (the new designation for a

Governor or Director) to make midnight or domiciliary visits, which ar eentirely unknown in the English County Asylums. Abuses of a grave character have, from time to time, come before the public, as occurring in some of the Private Asylums in England—not, however, in the public ones of that country, which possibly required such enactments as the foregoing— but in Ireland, with the experience of upwards of half a century, in the management of her Institutions, generally, for the Insane, no single act of cruelty or malapraxis or complaint is on record, in regard to their conduct, directly or indirectly ; and having thus long supported a character and place of the highest degree, it savours much of hardship and uncalled for penal severity, that any such degrading provisions, as those above referred to, should now be attempted to be made part and parcel of the law of the land.

DONATION TO THE ASYLUM.

A very gratifying circumstance came lately under the notice of the Board in regard to a former patient who, duly appreciating the benefit he had received whilst an inmate of the Institution, desired to present to its funds a sum of £20 in acknowledgment of the good services it had been happily instrumental in rendering to him. The Board, highly estimating this entirely voluntary act of generosity on the part of this former patient, found, however, that they could not receive it in the way proposed by the grateful donor; but it having been intimated to him that his wishes could be carried into effect by permitting the sum of money stated to be expended in some way that might be for the amusement and recreation of the patients, he at once gave his full approval to this suggestion ; and, accordingly, as it had been on a former occasion proposed that a self-acting organ would be a very desirable and soothing instrument to have for the patients, and one of that description being procurable for the above sum, the Board approved of the money so presented being allocated in the purchase thereof, and which, having since been obtained, the organ has been affording the greatest pleasure to the inmates generally. ———

The Resident Physician desires now, in conclusion, to tender his best thanks to the Governors for their continued kindness to him in the discharge of his duties, and also to express his acknowledgments to his brother officers for their valued aid at all times, as well as to record his satisfaction of the diligence and faithfulness of the attendants and domestics generally, in fulfilling the requirements of their respective onerous vocations.

ROBERT STEWART, M.D.,

RESIDENT PHYSICIAN.

BELFAST DISTRICT HOSPITAL FOR THE INSANE,
31st March, 1859.

APPENDIX (No. 1.)

GENERAL TABLES OF STATISTICS.

Table XVIII.—Shewing the Admissions, Discharges, &c., from each County in the District during the year ended 31st March, 1859.

ADMITTED FROM EACH COUNTY.

	Males.	Females.	Total.
Antrim, ...	29	26	55
County of the Town of Carrickfergus, ...	0	2	2
Down, ...	28	29	57
TOTALS, ...	57	57	114

DISCHARGED, &c., TO EACH COUNTY.

	Males.	Females.	Total.
Antrim, ...	27	22	49
County of the Town of Carrickfergus, ...	0	0	0
Down, ...	25	27	52
TOTALS, ...	52	49	101

REMAINING IN THE HOUSE, 31st MARCH, 1859.

	Males.	Females.	Total.
Antrim, ...	93	82	175
County of the Town of Carrickfergus, ...	3	6	9
Down, ...	102	71	173
TOTALS, ...	198	159	357

Table XIX.—Shewing the Per Centage of Discharges and Deaths, and the Average Per Centage, calculated on the Average Number of Patients for Thirteen Years, ended 31st March, 1859.

Years, ending 31st March.	Yearly Average Number.	RECOVERED.		RELIEVED.		DIED.	
		No. of Cases.	Rate Per Cent.	No. of Cases.	Rate Per Cent.	No. of Cases.	Rate Per Cent.
1847	254.96	60	23.58	22	8.62	27	9.51
1848	262.56	81	30.85	15	5.71	47	17.90
1849	271.32	69	25.43	14	5.16	30	11.05
1850	267.51	50	18.68	22	8.22	43	16.07
1851	271.12	81	29.87	29	10.69	29	10.69
1852	275.71	62	22.48	24	8.70	27	9.79
1853	280.01	67	23.92	21	7.49	25	8.92
1854	279.11	47	16.83	20	7.16	19	6.80
1855	266.48	36	13.50	21	7.88	39	14.63
1856	291.96	50	17.12	14	4.79	19	6.50
1857	323.25	66	20.41	15	4.64	39	11.75
1858	342.59	82	23.93	26	7.58	25	7.29
1859	347.21	65	18.17	18	5.18	18	5.18

Table XX.—Ages of the 357 Patients remaining in the Hospital on 31st March, 1859.

	Males.	Females.	Total.
Under 20 Years, ...	8	1	9
From 20 to 30 Years, ...	33	37	70
" 30 to 40 "	67	48	115
" 40 to 50 "	36	35	71
" 50 to 60 "	37	26	63
" 60 to 70 "	15	11	26
" 70 to 80 "	2	1	3
TOTALS, ...	198	159	357

Table XXI.—Shewing the Duration of Residence in the Hospital, of the 357 Patients remaining under Treatment, 31st March, 1859.

	Males.	Females.	Total.
From 1 to 2 Months, ...	7	4	11
" 2 to 3 "	2	5	7
" 3 to 6 "	9	7	16
" 6 to 9 "	11	8	19
" 9 Months to 1 Year, ...	5	5	10
" 1 Year to 18 Months, ...	20	13	33
" 18 Months to 2 Years, ...	6	12	18
" 2 Years to 4 "	33	32	65
" 4 " to 6 "	12	10	22
" 6 " to 10 "	30	26	56
" 10 " to 15 "	21	16	37
" 15 " to 20 "	16	12	28
" 20 " to 25 "	14	7	21
" 25 " to 30 "	12	2	14
TOTALS, ...	198	159	357

Table XXII.—Shewing the Articles Manufactured and made by the Patients during the year ended 31st March, 1859.

1,843 Hanks Linen Yarn.	30 Socks Footed.
200 Hanks Thread.	227 Shifts.
1,679 Yards Plain Linen.	157 Aprons.
36 Yards Twilled Linen.	110 Petticoats.
37 Yards Twilled Calico.	70 Wrappers.
274 Yards Ticken.	185 Day Caps.
71 Yards Diaper.	40 Bed Ticks.
160 Chequer.	50 Gowns.
630 Pairs Stockings and Socks.	143 Pillow Slips.
90 Pairs List Shoes Soled and Heeled.	386 Neck Ties.
	27 Quilted Blankets.
179 Sheets.	17 Rollers.
6 Men's Coats.	21 Overalls.
193 Shirts.	

Table XXIII.—Shewing the Number of Cases Admitted, Recovered, Relieved, and who Died in each Quarter and each Month, respectively, during the year ended 31st March, 1859:

| | Admitted. | | | Discharged. | | | | | | Died. | | |
| | | | | Recovered. | | | Relieved. | | | | | |
	Males.	Females.	Total.	Males.	Females.	Total.	Males.	Females.	Total.	Males.	Females.	Total.
April,	4	7	11	2	1	3	1	0	1	0	1	1
May,	2	2	4	4	2	6	0	2	2	0	2	2
June,	7	6	13	3	3	6	1	0	1	0	3	3
			—28			—15			—4			—6
July,	10	4	14	5	8	13	2	6	8	3	0	3
August,	6	8	14	2	1	3	1	2	3	1	0	1
September,	2	6	8	1	2	3	1	0	1	2	0	2
			—36			—19			—12			—6
October,	7	3	10	7	2	9	0	1	1	3	0	3
November,	8	8	16	1	4	5	0	0	0	1	0	1
December,	2	3	5	2	0	2	0	0	0	0	0	0
			—31			—16			—1			—4
January,	0	6	6	3	6	9	1	0	1	0	0	0
February,	6	2	8	3	2	5	0	0	0	0	0	0
March,	3	2	5	0	1	1	0	0	0	2	0	2
			—19			—15			—1			—2
	57	57	114	33	32	65	7	11	18	12	6	18

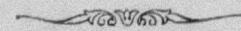

AN ACCOUNT OF THE RECEIPTS AND DISBURSEMENTS OF THE BELFAST DISTRICT HOSPITAL FOR THE INSANE, FOR ONE YEAR,

BEING FROM 1st APRIL, 1858, TO 31st MARCH, 1859.

THE CHARGE.

	£ s. d.	£ s. d.
Balance of last Account, in favour of the public, ..		1,039 18 0
Received from the Lords Commissioners of her Majesty's Treasury, ...		6,150 7 1
Received for Vegetables and Fruit sold,	38 8 6	
Do. Oats and Wheat sold, ..	47 8 3¾	
Do. Potatoes sold (diseased),	11 7 4½	
Do. Bones sold, ...	17 3 0	
Do. Fines on Servants,	0 10 0	
Do. Hay sold, ...	35 0 0	
Do. Grazing, ...	5 10 0	
Do. Cash unclaimed by Friends of a Patient, deceased,	4 3 0	
Do. Cash from the Insurance Offices, for damage sustained by Fire in Laundry,	270 0 0	
Do. Cash found on a Patient,	0 4 9	
Do. Cash error, in addition in Plumbing Account, ..	0 11 0	
	430 5 11	430 5 11
		£7,620 11 0
		£881 12 10
Balance in favour of the public, ...		£881 12 10

THE DISCHARGE.

	£ s. d.
Paid for Provisions, ...	£3,017 6 7
Do. Clothing, ...	665 3 5
Do. Bedding, ...	86 9 1
Do. Furniture, ...	66 9 7
Do. Fuel and Light, ...	366 9 11
Do. Soap, Candles, &c., ...	105 4 0
Do. Stationery and Printing, ..	40 0 0
Do. Advertising, ...	3 12 0
Do. Medicine, ...	10 15 5
Do. Repairs and Alterations, ..	783 5 3
Do. Farm and Garden Expenses, ..	55 8 7
Do. Insurance, ...	22 12 6
Do. Incidental Expenses, ...	69 10 2
Do. Salaries and Wages, ...	1,501 17 8
Do. Postage, ...	4 14 0
	£6,738 18 2
To Balance in hand, ...	881 12 10
	£7,620 11 0

AN ACCOUNT OF THE EXPENDITURE AND PRODUCE OF THE LAND OF THE BELFAST DISTRICT HOSPITAL FOR THE INSANE, FOR ONE YEAR, BEING FROM 1st APRIL, 1858, TO 31st MARCH, 1859.

Dr. — EXPENDITURE.

	£	s.	d.
To Seed Potatoes, ..	13	17	6
„ Seeds and Plants, ..	10	13	11
„ Spades, Hooks, Shovels, &c., ..	4	2	8
„ Shoeing Market Horse, ..	1	16	0
„ Rent Charge, ..	0	19	10
„ Saddlery Work, ..	12	12	0
„ Wheel Barrows, ..	1	12	0
„ Lime, ..	7	10	0
„ A New Market Cart, ..			
	£55	8	7
„ Balance, ..	310	13	5
Total, ..	£366	2	0

Cr. — PRODUCE.

	£	s.	d.	£	s.	d.
By 433¾ cwt. Potatoes, used in the Establishment, valued at 3s per cwt., ..	65	1	3			
„ 160 cwt. diseased do., sold at various prices, ..	11	7	4½	£76	8	7½
„ 90½ cwt. Oats, used in the Establishment, at 7s 6d per cwt., ..	32	16	7			
„ 57 cwt. do., sold at from 6s 7d to 7s 6d per cwt., ..	19	14	9¼	52	11	4¼
„ 62 cwt. Wheat, sold at from 9s 6d to 9s 3d per cwt., ..				27	13	6
„ 440 cwt. Straw, used in the Establishment, at 2s per cwt., ..				44	0	0
„ 200 cwt. Hay, used in the Establishment, at 2s 6d per cwt., ..	25	0	0			
„ 51 Cocks Hay, sold for ..	35	0	0	60	0	0
„ Vegetables and Fruit sold, ..	38	8	6			
„ Do. Used in the Establishment,	40	0	0	78	8	6
„ Manure, valued at ..				20	0	0
„ Osiers made into Baskets, ..				1	10	0
„ Grazing outside the Wall, ..				5	10	0
Total, ..				£366	2	0
„ Balance, ..				£310	13	5

DIETARY

OF

The Belfast District Hospital for the Insane.

BREAKFAST.

One quart stirabout (made with 8oz. fine or 7oz. coarse meal) and three-fourths of a pint mixed milk, ... } Males }
One-and-half pint stirabout and one-half pint mixed milk, ... } Females } Every Morning.

DINNER.

One-half pound loaf bread (or 3lbs. potatoes) six ounces solid meat, and one pint soup, ... } Males & Females } 3 days a-week.

One-half-pound loaf bread (or 3lbs. potatoes) and one quart soup (made with ox heads and bones cut out of meat, vegetables, oatmeal, barley, pease, &c.),... } Males }

One-half pound loaf bread (or 3lbs. potatoes) and one-and-half pint soup, ... } Females } 3 days a-week.

Three-fourths of a pound loaf bread (or 3½lbs. potatoes) and one pint mixed milk, ... } Males }

One-half pound loaf bread (or 3lbs. potatoes) and one pint mixed milk, ... } Females } 1 day a-week.

SUPPER.

One-half pound loaf bread and three-fourths of a pint of mixed milk, ... } Males }

One-half pound loaf bread and one-half pint mixed milk, ... } Females } Summer 6 months.

One quart stirabout and three-fourths of a pint new milk, ... } Males. }

One-and-half pint stirabout and one-half pint new milk, ... } Females } Winter 6 months.

₊ Patients who are actively employed are allowed a portion of meat, in addition to the soup, five instead of three days in the week. When the state of the patient's health requires it, the diet is changed accordingly, and any other substituted that may be considered requisite by the Medical Officers.

CORRESPONDENCE.

DISTRICT LUNATIC ASYLUM,
Belfast, February 11, 1859.

SIR,

I have been directed by the Governors respectfully to request that you will take the *earliest* opportunity of calling the *special* attention of his Excellency the Lord Lieutenant to the following serious errors contained in the Report of the Royal " Commissioners of Inquiry into the state of the Lunatic Asylums in Ireland," as presented to Parliament at the end of the last Session :—

The errors in question are at page 45 of the Commissioners' Report, in the Return " shewing the total of articles consumed in each of the several District Asylums for the year ended 25th December, 1856." In that Return, under the head of " Bread," the quantity given as consumed in this Asylum is but " 28,588lbs.," whereas it was nearly four times that amount —viz., 99,898lbs.

Again, as regards " Ox-heads" in the same Return, this Asylum has a blank attached to it ; whereas 797 were used, as duly stated to the Commissioners.

The Governors might also adduce another error (but of minor consequence) in the same Return, in respect to Tea, which is set down ten pounds *less* than it should have been ; but it is more particularly with reference to the " Bread" and " Ox-heads" that the Governors consider the entire official staff of the Institution to be most deeply compromised before Parliament, and the public generally, by the above extraordinary, and, to them, entirely unaccountable mistakes, on the part of the Royal Commissioners—mistakes which they now earnestly request His Excellency will be pleased to have *immediately* inquired into, and the correct statement made as public as the erroneous one has been.

The Governors feel the more strongly and deeply on this point, inasmuch as, at page 14 of the Commissioners' Report, the following extract, imputing nothing short of fraud, occurs, viz. :—" Copies of the Dietary Tables of Asylums, and of Returns shewing the consumption of the principal articles of food, will be found in the Appendix. These Returns, however, differ widely from the allowances specified in the diet tables of *some* Asylums, and *we cannot reconcile the apparent discrepancy.*

If the Returns of consumption are correct, the patients *cannot receive the amount of food professed to be allowed to them."*

The Governors have only to observe, with reference to the above quoted extract—the italics in which are their own—that, as regards the Belfast Asylum, "the apparent discrepancy" is at once acccounted for by the Commissioners' own palpably incorrect Return, and they now respectfully and firmly claim the right of having the unwarrantable imputation it contains against the administration of this Institution (implying both fraud and cruelty) *publicly* disclaimed. The Governors enclose herewith an extract from the Office Copy of the Return with which the Commissioners were supplied of the articles consumed here in 1856, as well as an extract from their own (the Commissioners) "table," so far as relates to the Belfast Asylum, of those articles, in order to shew how materially each differs, as has been already pointed out.—I am, sir, your most obedient servant,

(Signed)   R. STEWART, M.D.,
Resident Physician.

To Colonel Larcom, Under Secretary,
Dublin Castle.

[Extract as above referred to.]

BELFAST DISTRICT LUNATIC ASYLUM.

EXTRACT from Return to the Commissioners of the total quantities of the following articles consumed in the Asylum, for the year ending 25th December, 1856:—

	Tons.	Cwts.	Qrs.	Lbs.
Bread, ...	44	11	3	22
Ox-heads (797),	4	19	2	14
Tea, ...		3	1	10

Extract from Commissioners' Report—viz., p. 42, "No. 5 Table"—shewing the total quantities of the following articles consumed in each of the several District Lunatic Asylums for the year ending 25th December, 1856:—

BELFAST.   LBS.

	LBS.
Bread, ...	28,588
Ox-heads, ...	—
Tea, ...	364

(Signed)   R. STEWART, M.D.,
Resident Physician.

Belfast District Lunatic Asylum,
11th February, 1859.

SIR,

DUBLIN CASTLE,
18*th Feb.*, 1859.

I am directed by the Lord Lieutenant to acknowledge the receipt of your letter of the 11th instant, and its enclosure, relative to errors contained in the Report of the Royal Commissioners of Inquiry into the state of the Lunatic Asylums in Ireland.—I am, Sir, your obedient servant,

THOMAS LARCOM.

Robert Stewart, Esq., M.D., R.P.,
District Lunatic Asylum, Belfast.

SIR,

DISTRICT LUNATIC ASYLUM,
Belfast, Feb. 22, 1859.

At a Special Meeting of the Board of Governors, held here yesterday, directions were given to me to forward to you the enclosed copy of a letter, &c. (now printed for convenience), as transmitted by the Board to the Lord Lieutenant, with reference to the matter therein stated, the receipt of which has since been simply and formally acknowledged on the part of His Excellency, and to inform you that it was the unanimous desire of the Meeting that you and Sir H. Cairns, M.P., as members of the borough, be respectfully requested, at your earliest convenience, to inquire of Lord Naas, M.P., the Irish Secretary, in his place in the House of Commons, as to the existence of such a correspondence, and to call for its being laid before the House, and printed, with the view of such further proceedings being therewith taken as may be in accordance with the regulations of the House, the Governors all feeling that the subject of the letter is of the greatest and most serious moment to them, as a public body, vested with an important trust, as well as to the character of the Institution itself, and requiring, accordingly, to be prominently noticed and discussed before the House.—I am, Sir, your obedient Servant,

(Signed)

R. STEWART, M.D.,
Resident Physician.

To Richard Davison, Esq., M.P., 66, Warwick
Square, Belgrave Road, London.

DEAR SIR,

HOUSE OF COMMONS,
10*th March*, 1859.

At the request of Sir Hugh Cairns I have given notice to-night of my intention of moving to-morrow night for the correspondence with the Lord Lieutenant on the subject of the errors in the Commissioners Report. It will be unopposed, as I have got Lord Naas' consent for its production. —Very truly yours, R. DAVISON.

HOUSE OF COMMONS,
11th March, 1859.

My Dear Dr. Stewart,

When I wrote you yesterday evening I had not received your letter, which will account for the manner in which I commenced my letter. On my return home I got it; and to-day I have moved for the correspondence, to which Lord Naas assented.—Very truly yours,

R. DAVISON.

Belfast District Lunatic Ayslum.

At a Special Meeting of the Board of Governors of the Belfast District Lunatic Asylum, held in the Board-Room, on Monday, Feb. 21, 1859—the Very Rev. the Dean of Ross in the chair —a copy of the "Lunatic Poor (Ireland) Bill"—which was read a first time in the House of Commons, on the 7th instant —as introduced by the Right Honourable Lord Naas, Chief Secretary for Ireland, and the Right Honourable the Attorney-General for Ireland, having been laid before the Board, and many of its provisions appearing exceedingly objectionable in principle, and likely, if passed into law, to prove most injurious to the Lunatic Poor of Ireland, it was thereupon unanimously

Resolved—That a respectful application be made to Lord Naas and Mr. The Attorney-General for Ireland, to suspend all further proceedings in Parliament until the several Boards of Governors in Ireland shall have sufficient time for due consideration of the Bill; and, in particular, until this Board shall be able to confer with the Grand Juries of the Counties of Antrim, Down, and Carrickfergus, at the approaching Assizes.

That a copy of this resolution be sent to His Excellency the Lord Lieutenant of Ireland, the Members of Parliament for the Counties of Antrim, Down, and Carrickfergus; also, to the Members for Belfast, Lisburn, Downpatrick, and Newry; and that they be earnestly requested, without delay, to support the application of this Board to the Irish Secretary and the Attorney-General.

That copies be also transmitted to the several Boards of Governors of the other District Asylums in Ireland.

(Signed) JAMES STANNUS,
Chairman.

APPENDIX (No. 2.)

TO THE HONOURABLE

The Commons of Great Britain and Ireland,

IN PARLIAMENT ASSEMBLED.

The Humble Petition of the Board of Governors of the Belfast District Lunatic Asylum,

HUMBLY SHEWETH,

THAT your Petitioners are duly appointed GOVERNORS OF THE BELFAST DISTRICT LUNATIC ASYLUM, by the authority of the Lord Lieutenant and Privy Council of Ireland, agreeably to the provisions of the Act of 57 Geo. III., Cap. 106.

That this Institution has been in operation since the year 1829, having been established by virtue of the above-mentioned Act, for the maintenance and care of the Lunatic Poor of the Counties of Down and Antrim, and of the County of the Town of Carrickfergus.

That your Petitioners, taking a deep interest in all matters connected with the welfare of this Asylum, have read with much attention a Bill now before your honourable House, entitled the " Lunatic Poor (Ireland) Bill."

That your Petitioners, after maturely deliberating on the provisions of the above Bill, and after a lengthened experience from the closest attention to their duties, as Governors of the above Asylum, and a practical acquaintance with its progress, and great success, under the operation of the existing law, entertain grave objections to many of the provisions of the Bill before your honourable House, which appear to them exceedingly undesirable and, likely, if passed into law, greatly to impair the successful management of such Asylums, and to prove most injurious to the future interests of the Insane Poor of Ireland.

That the provisions of the Bill, appearing to have been largely drawn from the Lunacy Acts in operation in England, which are now before a Committee of your honourable House, to report upon, and for revision, your Petitioners humbly pray that you will be pleased to suspend the further progress of this measure, until, at all events, such Report shall be made, and the revision of the English Acts shall have been completed.

A Select Committee of your honourable House having been appointed to consider the provisions of " The Lunatic Poor (Ireland) Bill," your Petitioners have learned, with great regret, that said Committee has not yet obtained power to examine witnesses.

Your Petitioners, therefore, humbly pray, that, should your honourable House proceed with the said Bill, you will be pleased to grant power to the Committee so appointed, to summon witnesses, in order that your Petitioners may have an opportunity of submitting evidence in support of their strong objections to the Bill and its provisions, which have been stated, officially, to be based on the " Report of the Commissioners of Inquiry into the State of the Lunatic Asylums in Ireland"—a Report which contains, as your Petitioners are ready to prove, numerous and grave mis-statements, both direct and implied, in regard to this Institution ;

and, so far as your Petitioners understand, in regard to other similar Institutions in Ireland.

Your Petitioners view with alarm that any legislation, comprehending such an entire change in the administration of the Irish Asylums, should be based upon such Report; particularly from the course adopted by the Commissioners in taking evidence—a course which, Petitioners confidently submit, was not calculated to elicit such general information as to justify the extensive changes proposed, or to inspire confidence in the impartiality of the Commissioners; for, instead of constituting an open Court in Dublin, or some other central position, to obtain evidence of an efficient character, and have the same, and the opinions offered, scrutinised in such manner as might have led to sound practical results, the Commissioners adopted the plan of visiting each Asylum, and taking such evidence as was offered to them, not only local, but *ex-parte.*

Your Petitioners, deeply impressed with the importance of conducting the Inquiry in a public manner, as most likely to lead to beneficial results, did, on the 23rd October, 1856, and prior to such Inquiry being entered upon, address a letter to the Secretary of the said Commissioners, in which the following passage occurs:—

" We respectfully suggest, that, in order to render the labours of the Commissioners full, searching, and satisfactory, their Inquiries should be conducted under two great divisions—viz., one central, and the other local.

" The Central Investigation should, in our estimation, be held in Dublin, where parties nominated may attend, where evidence and statements shall be made in open Court, where the cross-examination of witnesses may be carried out by authorised representatives of the several Asylums, and where, through a searching public Inquiry, all important suggestions and information may be brought to bear upon the subject. The Local Investigation should, in our opinion, be held in each Asylum, the same principles of conducting the Inquiry, as above set forth, being fully recognised.

" We have thus ventured to indicate a course which, if adopted, would, in our judgment, be calculated to prove highly beneficial in relation to the general interests of the Irish Lunatic Asylums, and conclude by stating our firm conviction, that any investigation, conducted on principles less comprehensive, will be unsatisfactory to the public, who take a lively interest in the well-being of these establishments."

Instead of adopting the course thus respectfully suggested by Petitioners, the Commissioners merely held a Local Inquiry, and—in this Asylum, at least—declined permitting any cross-examination of witnesses, except by members of their own body. Consequently, Petitioners respectfully submit that any Report, upon an Inquiry so conducted, should not be acted upon without an opportunity to offer further evidence, with a view, in case of any change being made, to mature such a system of administration, as would be alike permanent and beneficial; and which Petitioners have reason to think would be the result, were the Select Committee so appointed empowered to take evidence thereon.

That such a Bill appears, in the mind of your Petitioners, and others, to be the more extraordinary from the fact that, whilst the laws of England, for the treatment of the Insane Poor, have worked so unsatisfactorily as to call forth a Committee of your honourable House, which is now sitting to receive evidence on, and report, it appears intended to base the changes of the laws of the Irish Asylums upon the English system, which will most probably be remodelled.

Your Petitioners, consequently, again most respectfully urge that, in case evidence be not received before the Select Committee now appointed for the consideration of " The Lunatic Poor (Ireland) Bill," that legislation in respect thereof be suspended, at least until the Report of the Committee on the English Lunacy Acts shall have been submitted to your honourable House.

Your Petitioners do not consider that the plan of placing the management and government of the Asylums of Ireland altogether in a Board of Visitors, chosen annually by the Grand Jury of each County, who are themselves a fluctuating body, nominated every half-year by the respective Sheriffs, (Officers annually appointed by the Crown), would afford satisfaction in the management of the important trusts of such Institutions, either to the public or the unhappily afflicted Inmates for whose benefit such Asylums have been established, inasmuch as the faithful discharge of the duties of such Visitors, which is of the most onerous and varied kind, would require years of practical experience to become acquainted with their performance, should not be largely subject to uncertainty or change.

That the Grand Jury system is, in itself, being subject to Parliamentary Revision, and likely, ere long, to be fundamentally changed; and your Petitioners submit that, until it shall be placed on a more permanent footing, the proposed legislation should be delayed.

That, should the contemplated Bill pass into a law, there would not be the same Parliamentary or public control over the conduct of Visitors appointed under the proposed Act; nor would they, as a body, subject to annual fluctuation, have the same interest in the management, or be under the same responsibility, as those whose appointment would be more permanent, as it is under the present system.

Further, having seen, by the public papers, that serious imputations have been cast upon the management and condition of the District Lunatic Asylums throughout Ireland generally, and those imputations having been founded on the Report of the Commissioners, your Petitioners, on this account, specially appeal to the justice of your honourable House to be permitted to offer evidence before the Committee in refutation of those imputations, most injuriously and unfoundedly affecting—by implication, at least—the Asylum under your Petitioners charge, to which, by their attendance on Board Meetings and vigilant inspections, they have devoted—as public and official records will prove—the greatest and most persevering care.

Your Petitioners humbly solicit the attention of your honourable House to the fact that, so far from the District Asylums in Ireland having failed, as the Commissioners insinuate, to effect the objects for which they were established, it has been recently shewn, from a source the most disinterested as well as of the highest professional authority in these countries in all matters connected with Insanity—namely — *The Quarterly Journal of Psychological Medicine*, edited by Dr. Forbes Winslow, that, after an examination of the Returns given in the very Report of the Commissioners of Inquiry, the Irish District Asylums bear the most favourable comparison with the English County Asylums, as to recoveries and deaths—the true tests of the successful working of such Institutions.

In confirmation of the foregoing statement, your Petitioners give the following extract from the above-named publication, contained in its issue for the month of January, 1859, viz. :—

" It is a somewhat singular fact, that, while the Commissioners have, throughout their Report, kept constantly the great proposition in view that an Asylum should be an Institution for the treatment, as well as for the retention of the insane, they should have altogether passed over, without observation, the data submitted to them, and printed by them, in the Appendix to the Report, which indicate the character of the Asylums of Ireland as curative Institutions for the Insane. When these data—so important to a right knowledge of the subject of investigation—are examined, a suspicion is excited that the generally unfavourable opinion of the Commissioners upon the District Asylums arises, in no small degree, from their having raised a false standard of comparison. We do not desire, for a moment, to convey an impression that we in any way approve, or would wish the continuance of those irregularities and defects in management that the Commissioners report; but the omission upon their part of any allusion to the most creditable, as well as most important feature of the Asylum returns is a circumstance much to be regretted.

" From the tables of admissions and discharges of the different District Asylums, it would appear that the proportion of recoveries, calculated on the admissions, for the whole of the District Asylums, on an average of five years (1852-56), was 39·2 per cent.; and that the mortality of the same Asylums, calculated upon the whole number of insane within them, during the same period, was 10·5 per cent. These proportions, both of recoveries and deaths, compare very favourably with those occurring in English County Asylums, the mortality being below, and the recoveries almost equal to, the proportions found in those Institutions."

That, until the year 1854, when Chaplains were admitted into this Asylum, in deference to the wish of the Lord Lieutenant of Ireland, this Institution stood very considerably in advance of any in Ireland, having Chaplains, in its per centage of cases cured and relieved.

During the two years, however, in which Chaplains officiated herein, from the excitement produced by their attendance on the Patients, and other causes connected therewith, the per centage of cures became diminished to the extent of one-third at least; but, since the discontinuance of Chaplains for the last three years, this Institution has recovered its distinguished position in regard to the number of those cured and relieved.

Petitioners, therefore, without desiring to interfere with the management of other Asylums, most respectfully solicit that, in any Bill which may pass your honourable House, the appointment of Chaplains shall be left exclusively to the discretion of the Board of Governors for the time being—in making which request they are sustained by the repeated and unanimous declarations of the Grand Juries of the three Counties with which this Asylum is connected.

Your Petitioners, nevertheless, deeply sensible of the great value of the existing public Institutions for the Insane in Ireland, and of their usefulness being increased, do not hesitate to admit that they are susceptible of improvement in several respects; especially in regard to a better classification of patients and other important matters.

Your Petitioners, accordingly, are most desirous to see their benevolent objects carried out to the fullest available extent.

Therefore, for the foregoing and other cogent reasons, your Petitioners again humbly pray, that your honourable House will stay the further progress of "The Lunatic Poor (Ireland) Bill," give power to the Select Committee to summon witnesses in regard to its provisions, and permit your Petitioners to defend their own Institution against the heavy charges which have

14. *Derbyshire Do.*, reports for 1856—'57, pp. 15 and 30.—By John Hitchman, M.D., Physician-Superintendent.
15. *Dorset Do. (at Forston)*, annual reports for 1856—'57, pp. 43 and 36.—By J. G. Symes, M.R.C.S., Eng., Surgeon-Superintendent.
16. *Essex Do.*, reports for 1856-'57-'58.—By D. C. Campbell, M.D., Physician-Superintendent.
17. *Kent Do. (at Barming-Heath, Maidstone)*, annual report, to 4th July, 1858, pp. 31.—By James E. Huxley, M.D., Physician-Superintendent.
18. *Lancaster Do.*, annual report for 1857, pp. 37.—By John Broadhurst, M.R.C.S., Eng., Surgeon-Superintendent.
19. *Lancashire Do. (at Rainhill)*, annual report for 1857, pp. 69.—By John D. Cleaton, M.R.C.S., Eng., Surgeon-Superintendent.
20. *Lancashire Do. (at Prestwich)*, do. do., By J. Holland, F.R.C.S., Eng., Surgeon-Superintendent.
21. *Lincolnshire Do. (at Bracebridge)*, fifth annual report for 1857, pp. 32. —By Edward Palmer, M.D., Physician-Superintendent.
22. Metropolitan Commissioners in Lunacy, twelfth report, to 31st March, 1858, pp. 56.
23. *Middlesex Do. (at Colney Hatch)*, annual report for 1857, pp. 194.— By D. F. Tyerman and W. G. Marshall, Surgeon-Superintendents.
24. *Nottingham County and Borough Do.*, forty-sixth annual report for 1858, pp. 27.—By W. P. Stiff, M.B., Physician-Superintendent.
25. *Oxford and Berks Do. (at Littlemore)*, annual reports for 1857-'58, pp. 42 and 29.— By William Ley, M.R.C.S., Eng., Surgeon-Superintendent.
26. Plea in favour of the Insane Poor, pp. 11.— By John Miller, F.R.C.S., Edinburgh, Medical-Superintendent, Bethnall House Asylum.
27. *Suffolk Do. (at Melton Woodbridge)*, annual report for 1858, pp. 36.— By J. Kirkman, M.D., Physician-Superintendent.
28. *Warneford Do. (at Oxford)*, sheet reports, 1856-'57.— By T. Allen, M.R.C.S., Eng., Surgeon-Superintendent.
29. *Wilts Do. (at Devizes)*, seventh annual report, for 1857, pp. 44.—By John Thurnam, M.D., Physician-Superintendent.
30. *Worcester Do.*, reports for 1856-'57, pp. 76.—By James Sherlock, M.D., Physician-Superintendent.

Scotch.

31. *Aberdeen Royal Hospital for the Insane*, annual report, to 31st Dec., 1857, pp. 24.—By Robert Jamieson, M.D., Physician-Superintendent.
32. *Crichton Royal Institution Do. (at Dumfries)*, eighteenth annual report, to 11th November, 1857, pp. 44.—By W. A. F. Browne, M.D., Physician-Superintendent.
33. *Dundee Royal Hospital Do.*, thirty-eighth annual report, to 16th June, 1858, pp. 35.—By T. T. Wingett, M.D.

34. *Edinburgh Do. (at Morningside)*, annual report for 1857, pp. 44.—By D. Skae, M.D., Physician-Superintendent.
35. Edinburgh House and School for Invalids and Imbecile Children, report for 1857, pp. 8.—David Brodie, M.D., Medical-Superintendent.
36. *Glasgow Do.*, forty-fourth annual report, for 1857, pp. 52.—By Alex. Mackintosh, M.D., Physician-Superintendent.
37. "Morningside Mirror," monthly periodical, conducted by the inmates of the above establishment.
38. *Montrose Do.*, annual reports, 1849-'58.—By James C. Howden, M.D., Physician-Superintendent.
39. *Perth (James Murray's) Do.*, thirty-first annual report, to June, 1858.— By L. Lindsay, M.D., Physician-Superintendent.

American.

40. Hartford Retreat, Conn., thirty-second and thirty-third annual reports, to 31st March, 1856-'57, pp. 32 and 31.—By John S. Butler, M.D., Physician-Superintendent.
41. *Massachussetts*, report of the causes of Idiocy.—By S. G. Howe, M.D., and others.
42. *Massachussetts*, report of Insanity, pp. 79.—By Edward Jarvin, M.D., Dorchester.
43. *Michigan State Asylum*, reports for 1855-'56, pp. 70.—By Edwin H. Van Deusen, M.D., Physician-Superintendent.
44. *Toronto Provincial Asylum for the Insane (Western Canada)*, annual report, to 1st March, 1858.—By Joseph Workman, M.D., Physician-Superintendent.

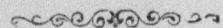

PRINTED AT
THE DAILY NORTHERN WHIG OFFICE,
BELFAST.